POWER CODERS

THE SECRET OF THE FIVE BUGS

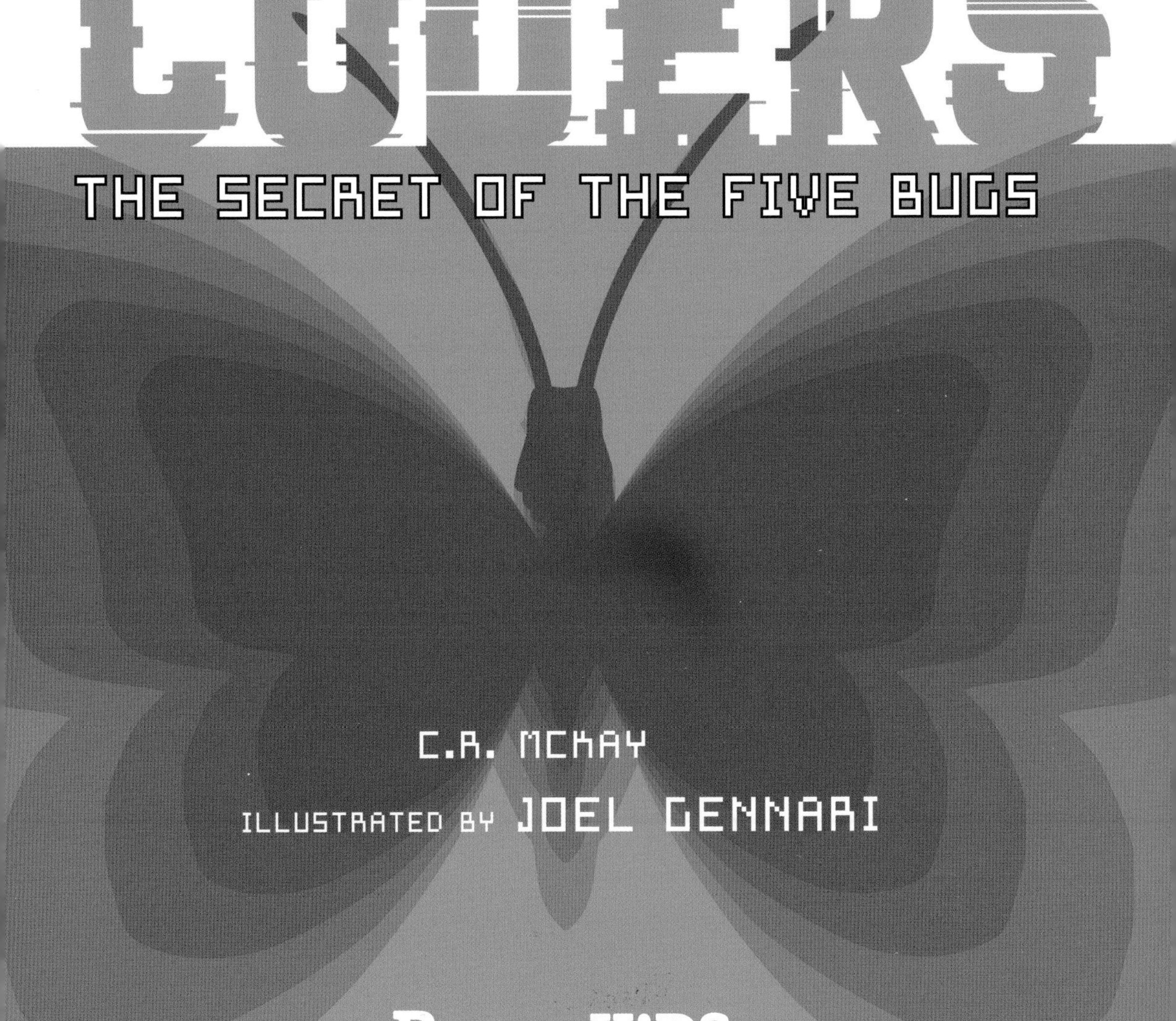

C.R. MCKAY
ILLUSTRATED BY JOEL GENNARI

PowerKiDS press
New York

Published in 2019 by The Rosen Publishing Group, Inc.
29 East 21st Street, New York, NY 10010

First Edition

Illustrator: Joel Gennari
Interior Layout: Tanya Dellaccio
Managing Editor: Nathalie Beullens-Maoui
Editorial Director: Greg Roza

Cataloging-in-Publication Data

Names: McKay, C.R.
Title: The secret of the five bugs / C.R. McKay.
Description: New York : PowerKids Press, 2019. | Series: Power coders
Identifiers: LCCN ISBN 9781538340141 (pbk.) | ISBN 9781538340134 (library bound) | ISBN 9781538340158 (6 pack)
Subjects: LCSH: Computer programming–Juvenile fiction. | Computer science–Juvenile fiction. | Insects–Juvenile fiction.
Classification: LCC PZ7.1.M43543 Se 2019 | DDC [E]–dc23

Manufactured in the United States of America

CPSIA Compliance Information: Batch CS18PK: For Further Information contact Rosen Publishing, New York, New York at 1-800-237-9932

CONTENTS

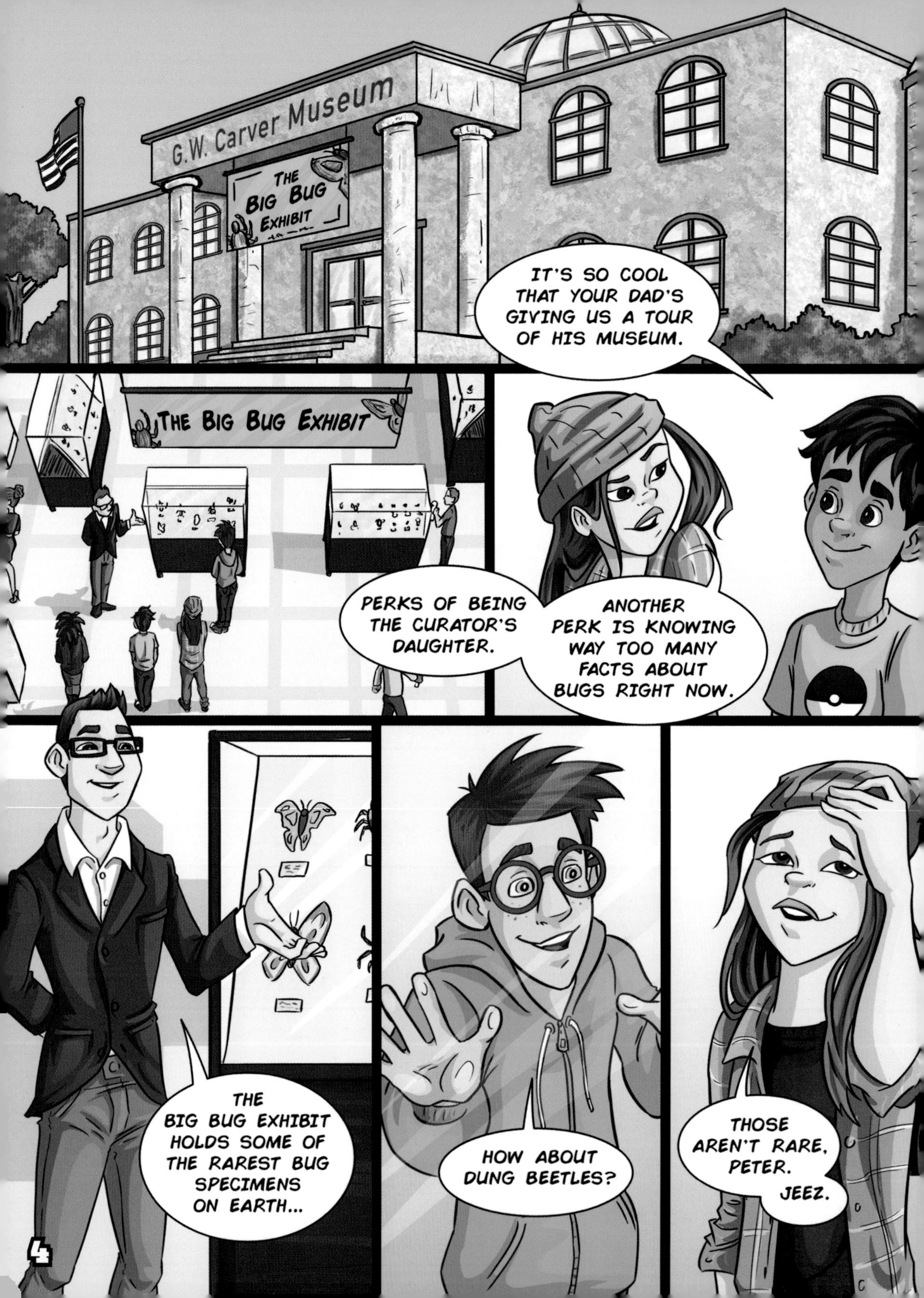
G.W. Carver Museum
THE BIG BUG EXHIBIT
IT'S SO COOL THAT YOUR DAD'S GIVING US A TOUR OF HIS MUSEUM.
THE BIG BUG EXHIBIT
PERKS OF BEING THE CURATOR'S DAUGHTER.
ANOTHER PERK IS KNOWING WAY TOO MANY FACTS ABOUT BUGS RIGHT NOW.
THE BIG BUG EXHIBIT HOLDS SOME OF THE RAREST BUG SPECIMENS ON EARTH...
HOW ABOUT DUNG BEETLES?
THOSE AREN'T RARE, PETER.
JEEZ.

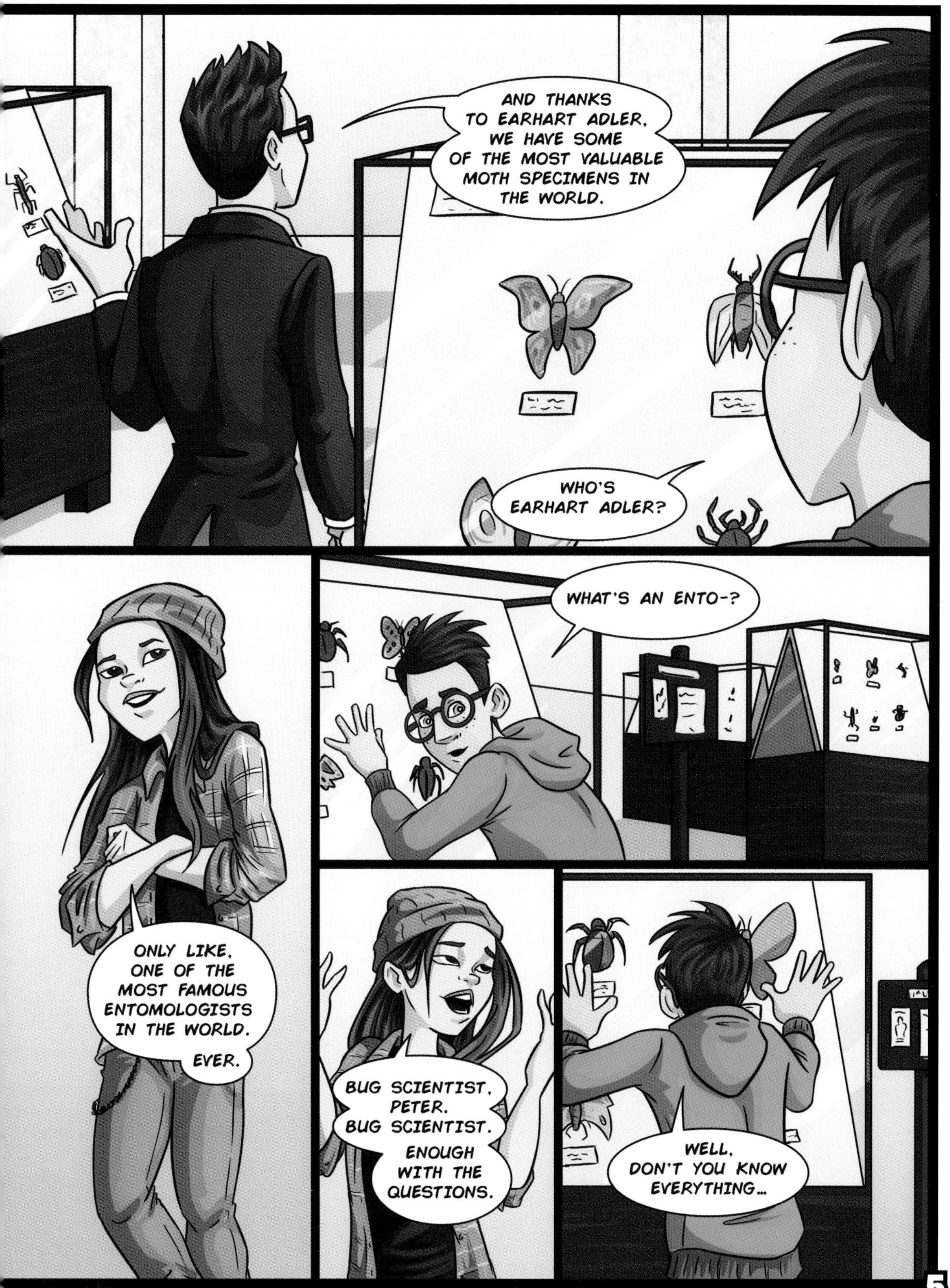
AND THANKS TO EARHART ADLER, WE HAVE SOME OF THE MOST VALUABLE MOTH SPECIMENS IN THE WORLD.
WHO'S EARHART ADLER?
ONLY LIKE, ONE OF THE MOST FAMOUS ENTOMOLOGISTS IN THE WORLD.
EVER.
WHAT'S AN ENTO-?
BUG SCIENTIST, PETER. BUG SCIENTIST.
ENOUGH WITH THE QUESTIONS.
WELL, DON'T YOU KNOW EVERYTHING...

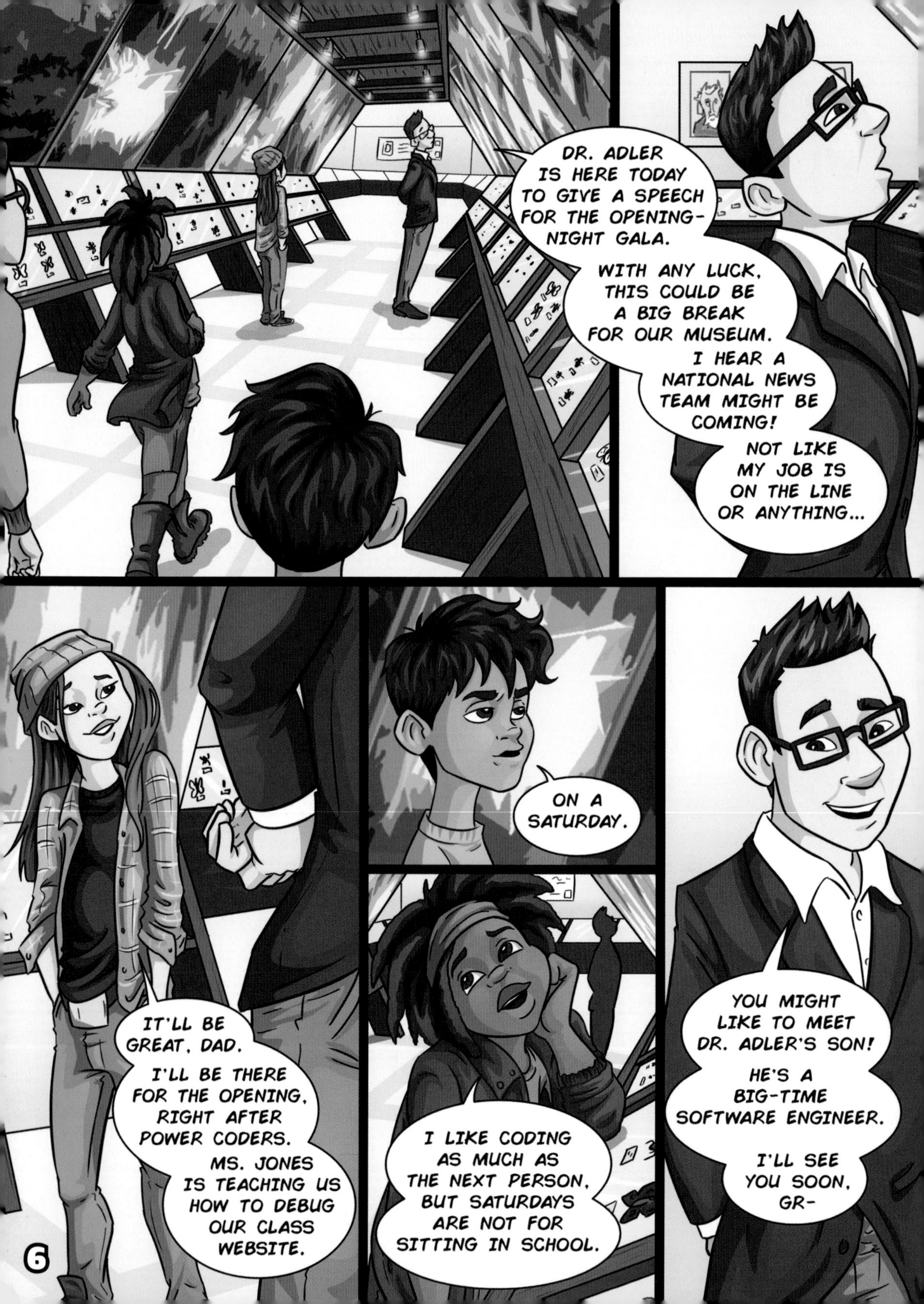
DR. ADLER IS HERE TODAY TO GIVE A SPEECH FOR THE OPENING-NIGHT GALA.
WITH ANY LUCK, THIS COULD BE A BIG BREAK FOR OUR MUSEUM.
I HEAR A NATIONAL NEWS TEAM MIGHT BE COMING!
NOT LIKE MY JOB IS ON THE LINE OR ANYTHING...
IT'LL BE GREAT, DAD.
I'LL BE THERE FOR THE OPENING, RIGHT AFTER POWER CODERS.
MS. JONES IS TEACHING US HOW TO DEBUG OUR CLASS WEBSITE.
ON A SATURDAY.
I LIKE CODING AS MUCH AS THE NEXT PERSON, BUT SATURDAYS ARE NOT FOR SITTING IN SCHOOL.
YOU MIGHT LIKE TO MEET DR. ADLER'S SON!
HE'S A BIG-TIME SOFTWARE ENGINEER.
I'LL SEE YOU SOON, GR-

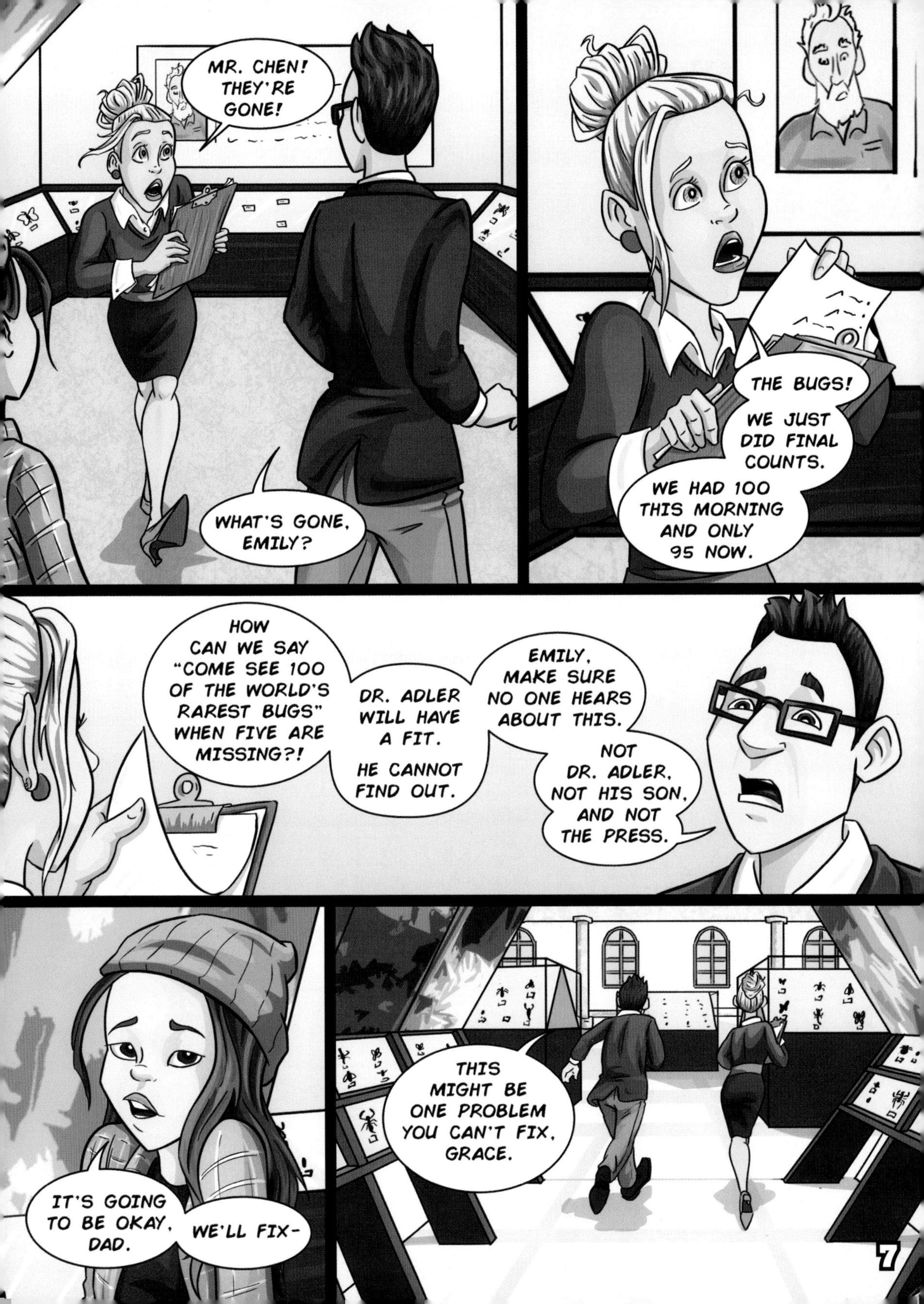
MR. CHEN! THEY'RE GONE!
WHAT'S GONE, EMILY?
THE BUGS!
WE JUST DID FINAL COUNTS.
WE HAD 100 THIS MORNING AND ONLY 95 NOW.
HOW CAN WE SAY "COME SEE 100 OF THE WORLD'S RAREST BUGS" WHEN FIVE ARE MISSING?!
DR. ADLER WILL HAVE A FIT.
HE CANNOT FIND OUT.
EMILY, MAKE SURE NO ONE HEARS ABOUT THIS.
NOT DR. ADLER, NOT HIS SON, AND NOT THE PRESS.
IT'S GOING TO BE OKAY, DAD.
WE'LL FIX-
THIS MIGHT BE ONE PROBLEM YOU CAN'T FIX, GRACE.

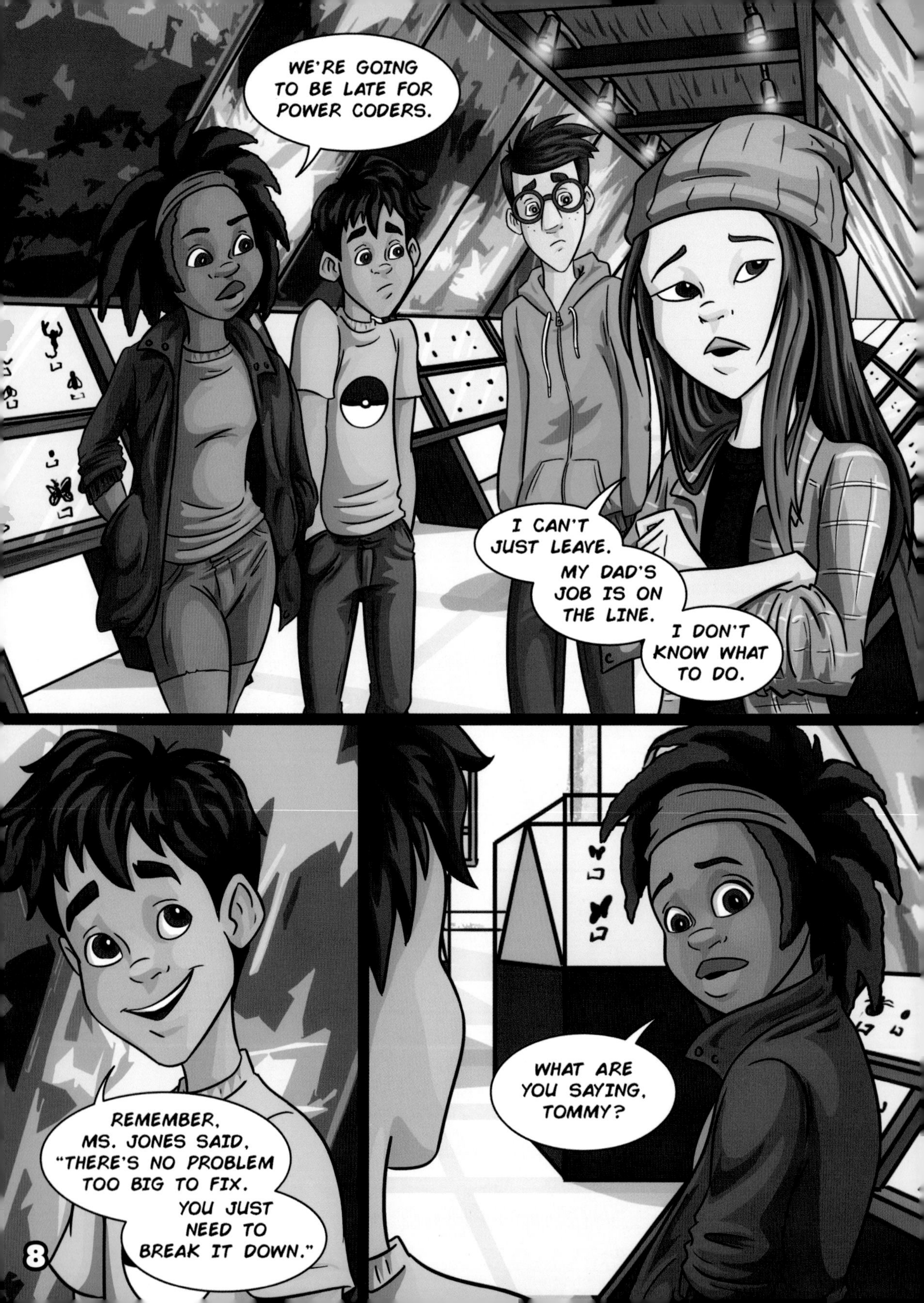
WE'RE GOING TO BE LATE FOR POWER CODERS.
I CAN'T JUST LEAVE. MY DAD'S JOB IS ON THE LINE. I DON'T KNOW WHAT TO DO.
REMEMBER, MS. JONES SAID, "THERE'S NO PROBLEM TOO BIG TO FIX. YOU JUST NEED TO BREAK IT DOWN."
WHAT ARE YOU SAYING, TOMMY?

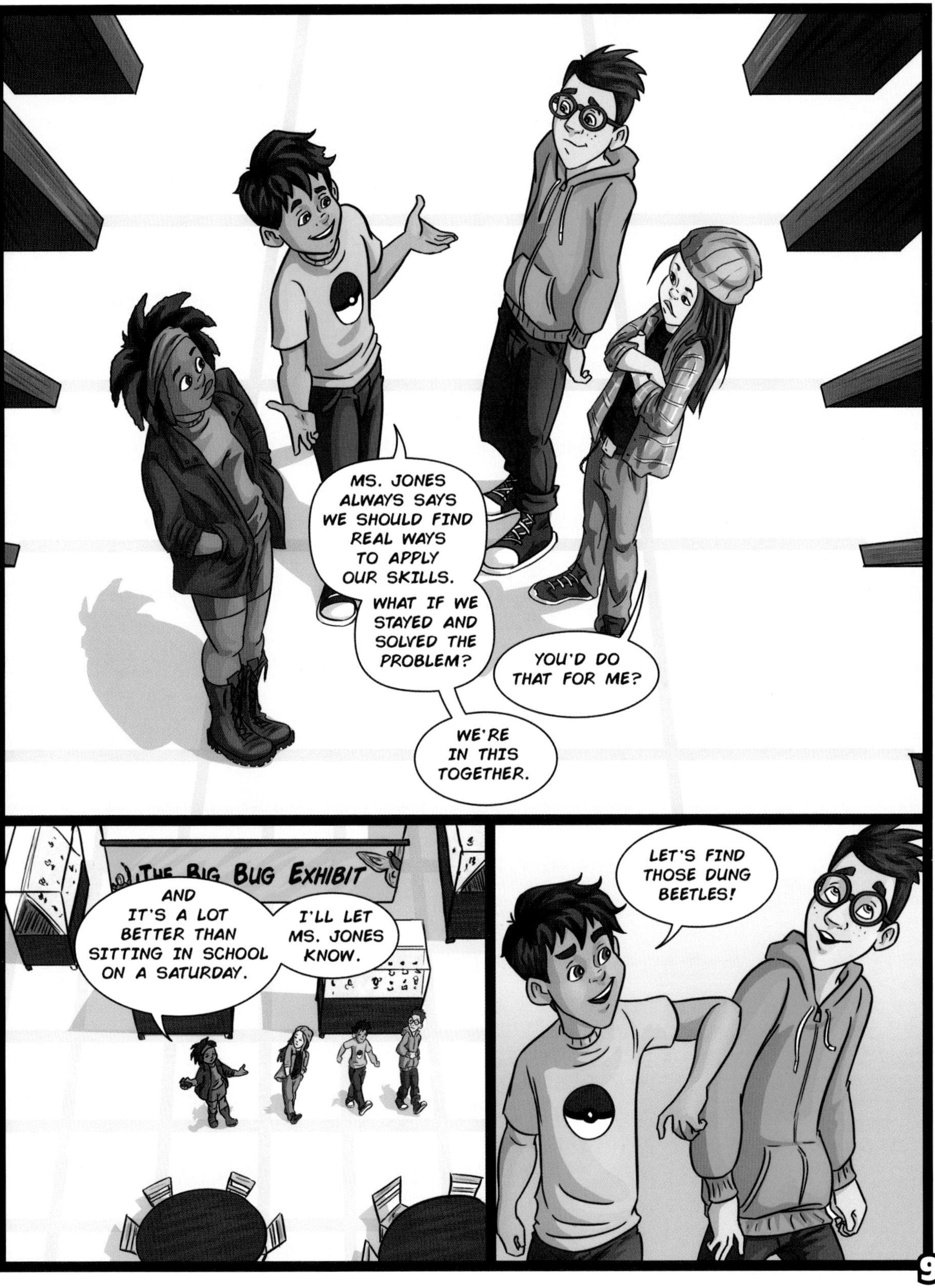
MS. JONES ALWAYS SAYS WE SHOULD FIND REAL WAYS TO APPLY OUR SKILLS.
WHAT IF WE STAYED AND SOLVED THE PROBLEM?
YOU'D DO THAT FOR ME?
WE'RE IN THIS TOGETHER.
THE BIG BUG EXHIBIT
AND IT'S A LOT BETTER THAN SITTING IN SCHOOL ON A SATURDAY.
I'LL LET MS. JONES KNOW.
LET'S FIND THOSE DUNG BEETLES!

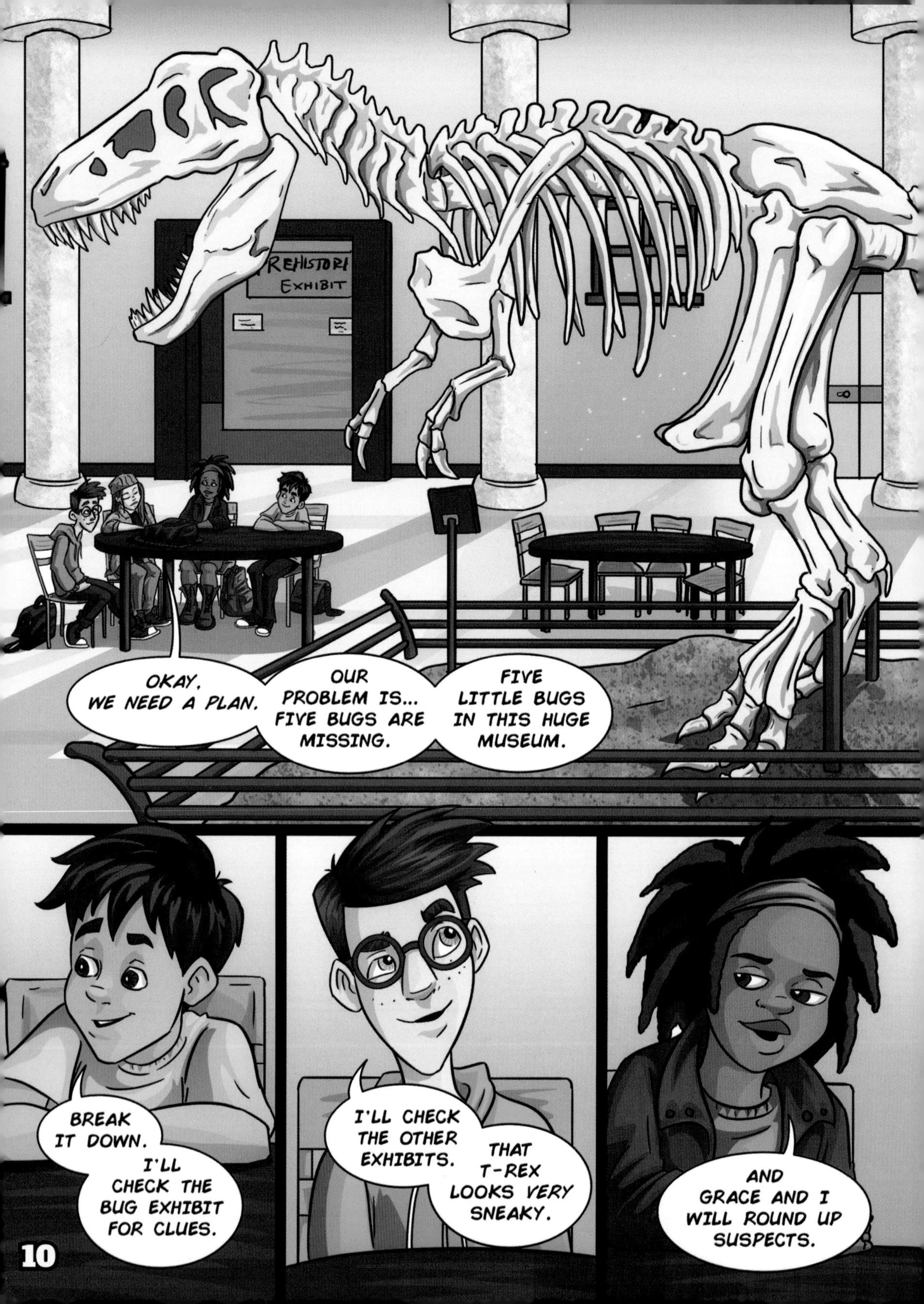
REHISTORI
EXHIBIT
OKAY, WE NEED A PLAN.
OUR PROBLEM IS... FIVE BUGS ARE MISSING.
FIVE LITTLE BUGS IN THIS HUGE MUSEUM.
BREAK IT DOWN.
I'LL CHECK THE BUG EXHIBIT FOR CLUES.
I'LL CHECK THE OTHER EXHIBITS.
THAT T-REX LOOKS VERY SNEAKY.
AND GRACE AND I WILL ROUND UP SUSPECTS.

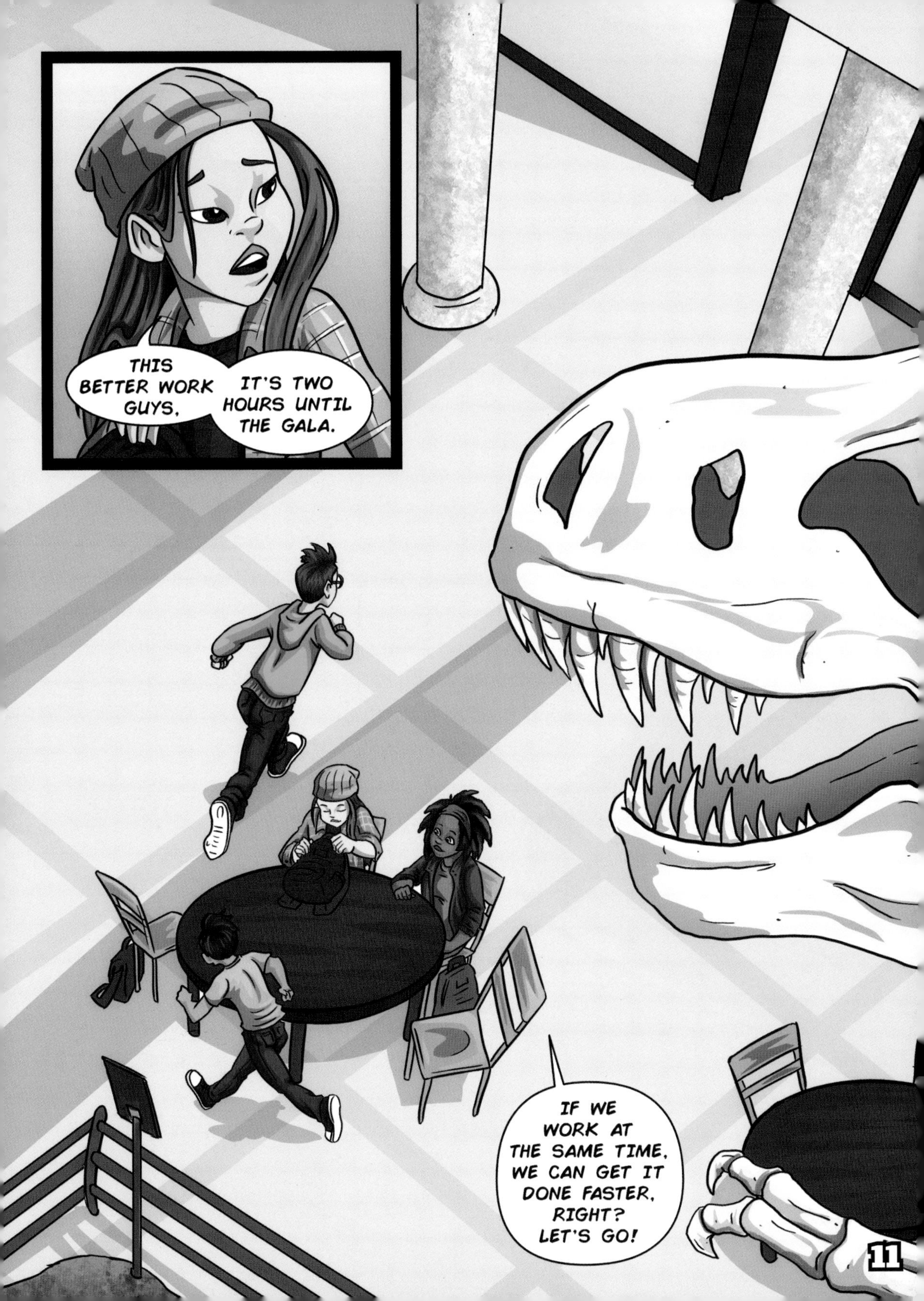
THIS BETTER WORK GUYS.
IT'S TWO HOURS UNTIL THE GALA.
IF WE WORK AT THE SAME TIME, WE CAN GET IT DONE FASTER, RIGHT? LET'S GO!

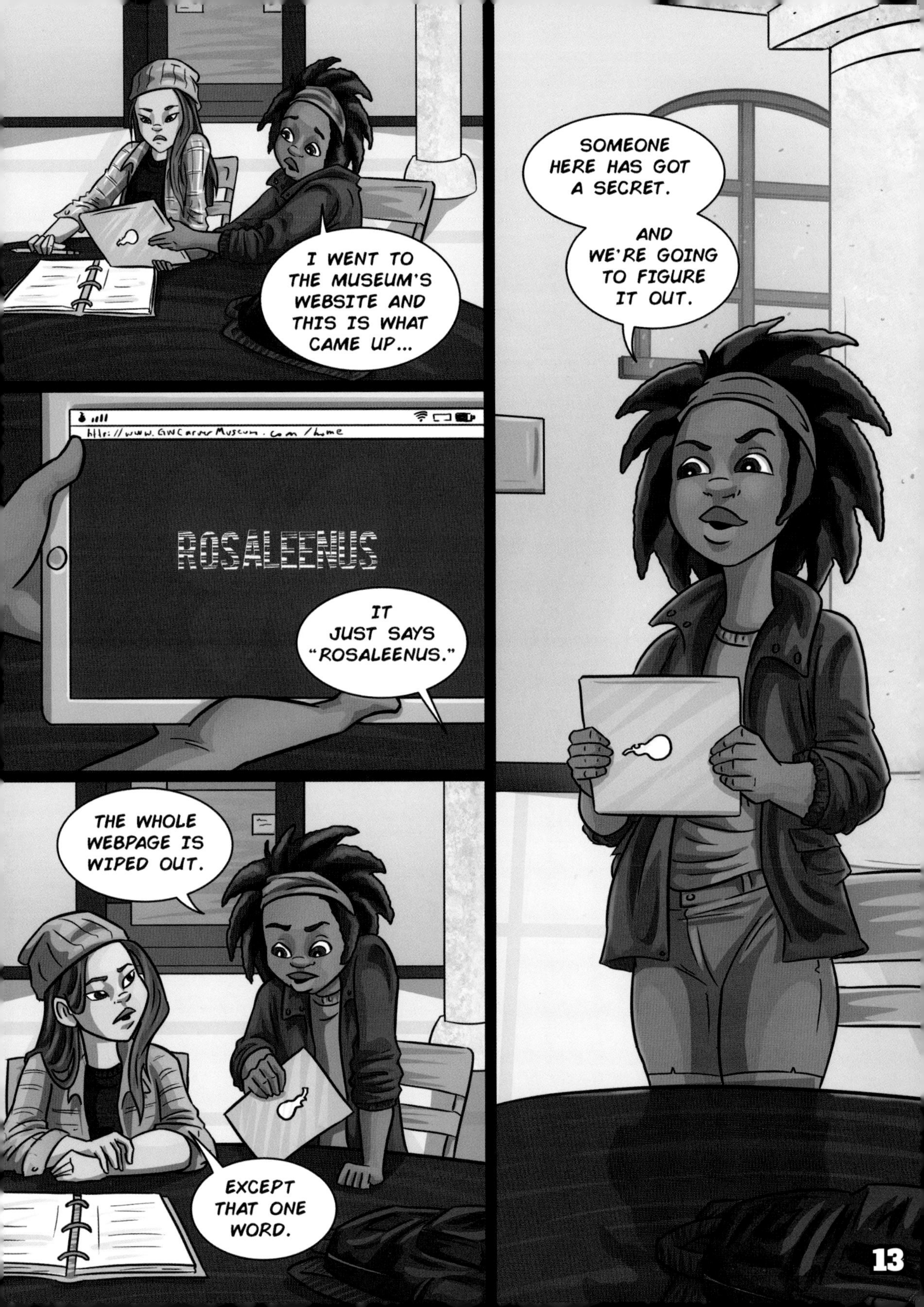

I WENT TO THE MUSEUM'S WEBSITE AND THIS IS WHAT CAME UP...
ROSALEENUS
IT JUST SAYS "ROSALEENUS."
THE WHOLE WEBPAGE IS WIPED OUT.
EXCEPT THAT ONE WORD.
SOMEONE HERE HAS GOT A SECRET.
AND WE'RE GOING TO FIGURE IT OUT.

AAAHHHHHHH!!!

THE BIG BUG EXHIBIT
R...BUGS

BIG BU
EXHIBIT
RE BUGS

THE BIG BU
EXHIBIT
BUGS

THAT WAS A CLOSE ONE.

BINGO.

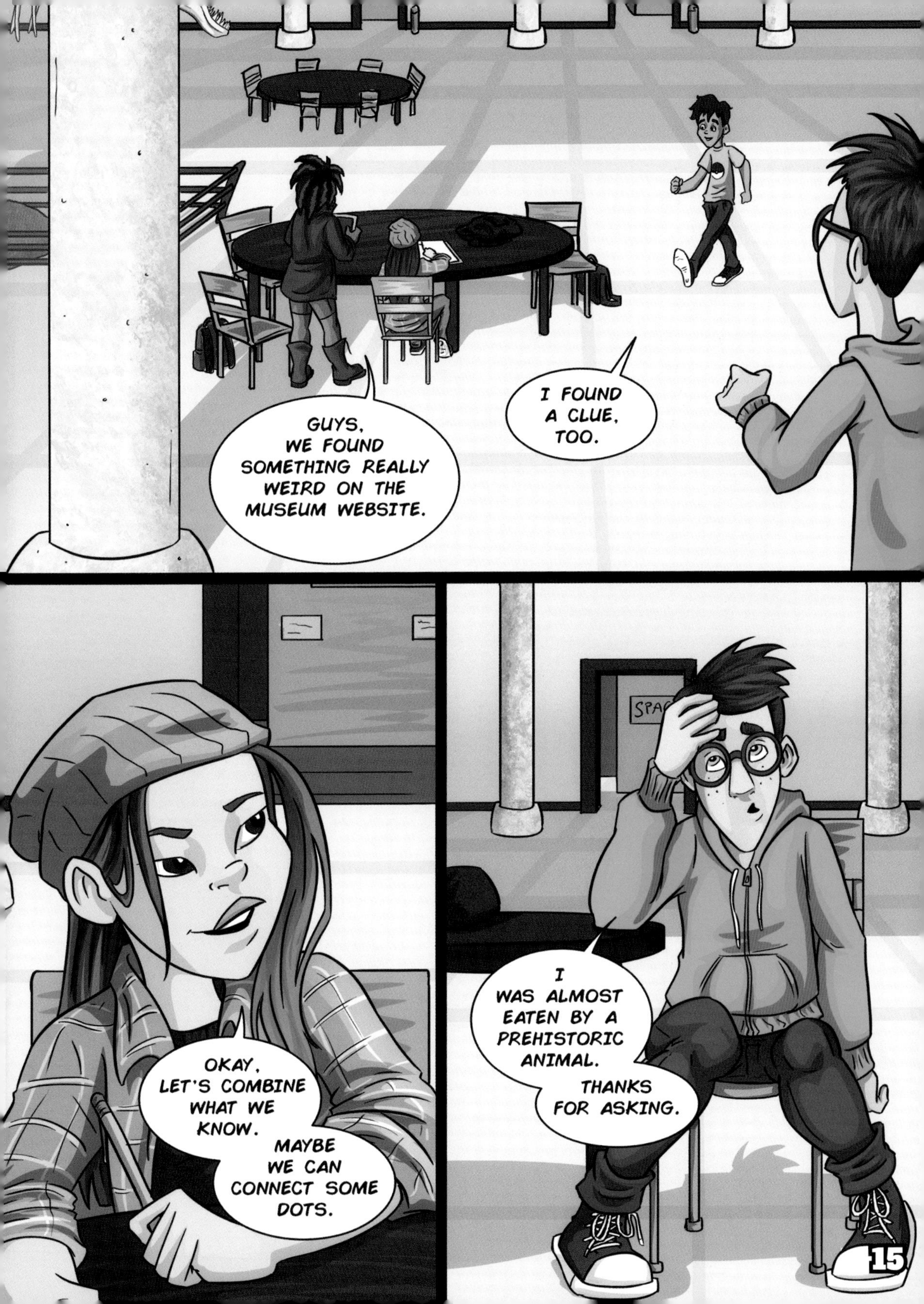

GUYS, WE FOUND SOMETHING REALLY WEIRD ON THE MUSEUM WEBSITE.
I FOUND A CLUE, TOO.
SPAC
OKAY, LET'S COMBINE WHAT WE KNOW.
MAYBE WE CAN CONNECT SOME DOTS.
I WAS ALMOST EATEN BY A PREHISTORIC ANIMAL.
THANKS FOR ASKING.

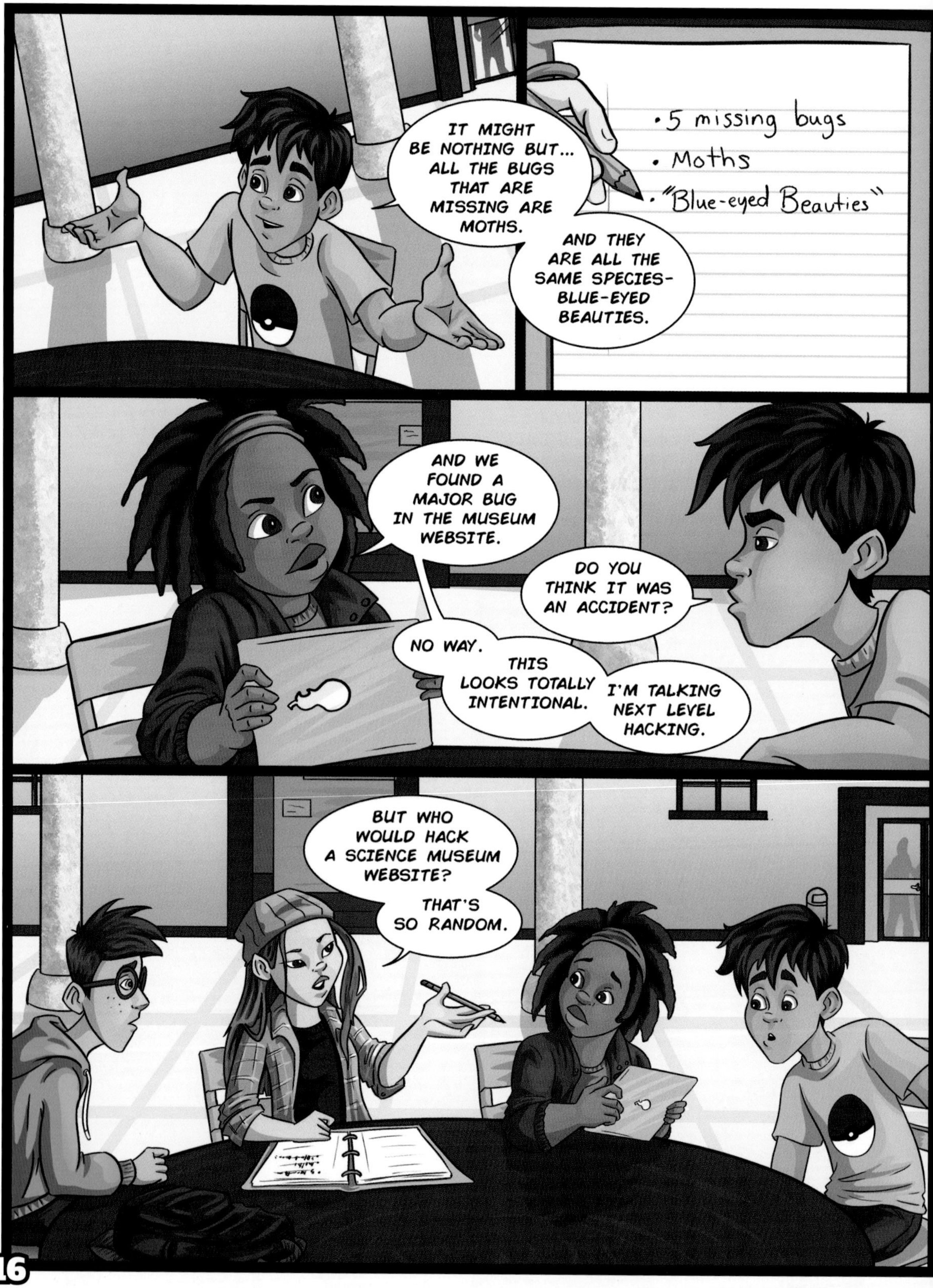
IT MIGHT BE NOTHING BUT... ALL THE BUGS THAT ARE MISSING ARE MOTHS.
•5 missing bugs
• Moths
• "Blue-eyed Beauties"
AND THEY ARE ALL THE SAME SPECIES- BLUE-EYED BEAUTIES.
AND WE FOUND A MAJOR BUG IN THE MUSEUM WEBSITE.
DO YOU THINK IT WAS AN ACCIDENT?
NO WAY.
THIS LOOKS TOTALLY INTENTIONAL.
I'M TALKING NEXT LEVEL HACKING.
BUT WHO WOULD HACK A SCIENCE MUSEUM WEBSITE?
THAT'S SO RANDOM.

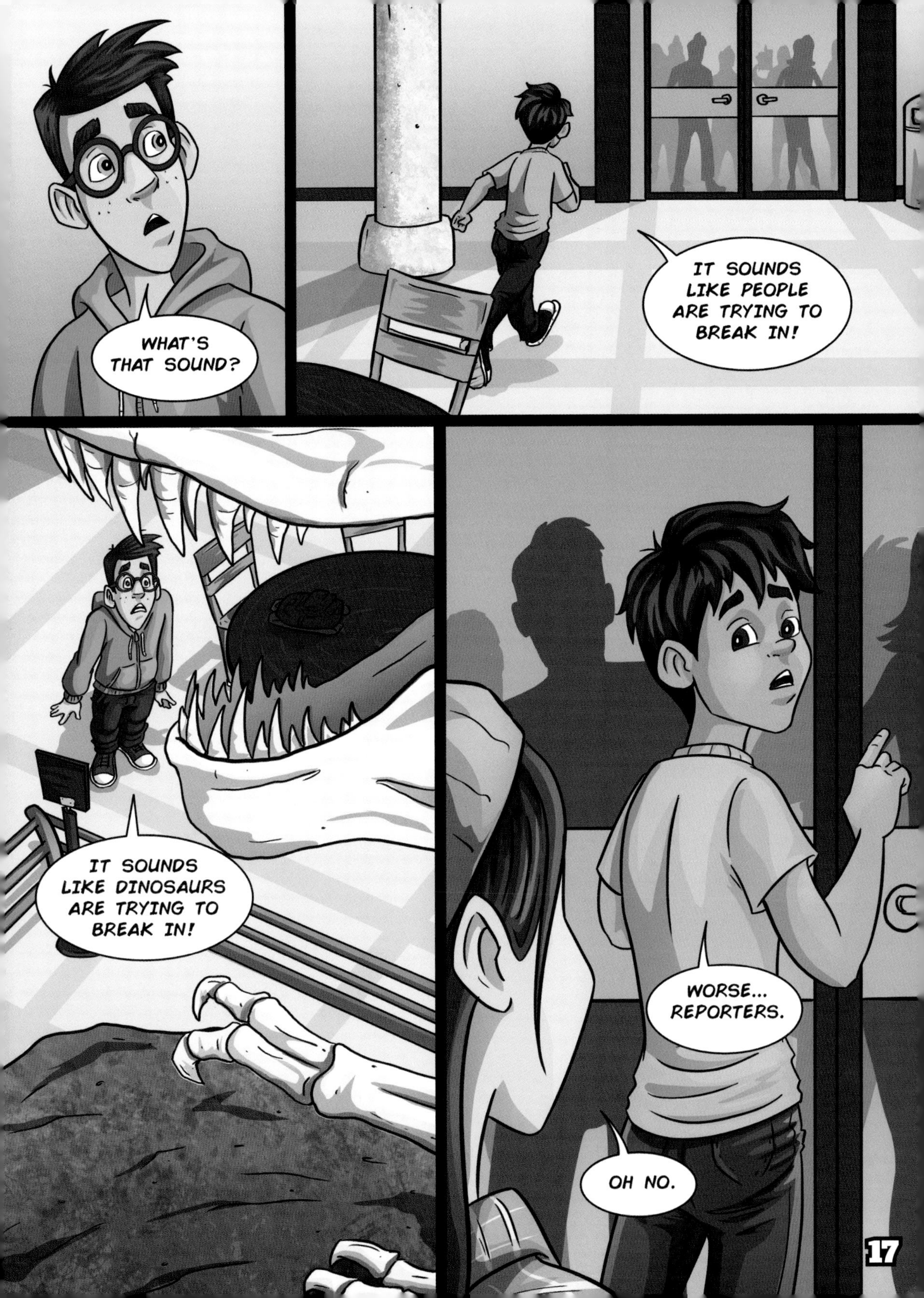
WHAT'S THAT SOUND?
IT SOUNDS LIKE PEOPLE ARE TRYING TO BREAK IN!
IT SOUNDS LIKE DINOSAURS ARE TRYING TO BREAK IN!
WORSE... REPORTERS.
OH NO.

19

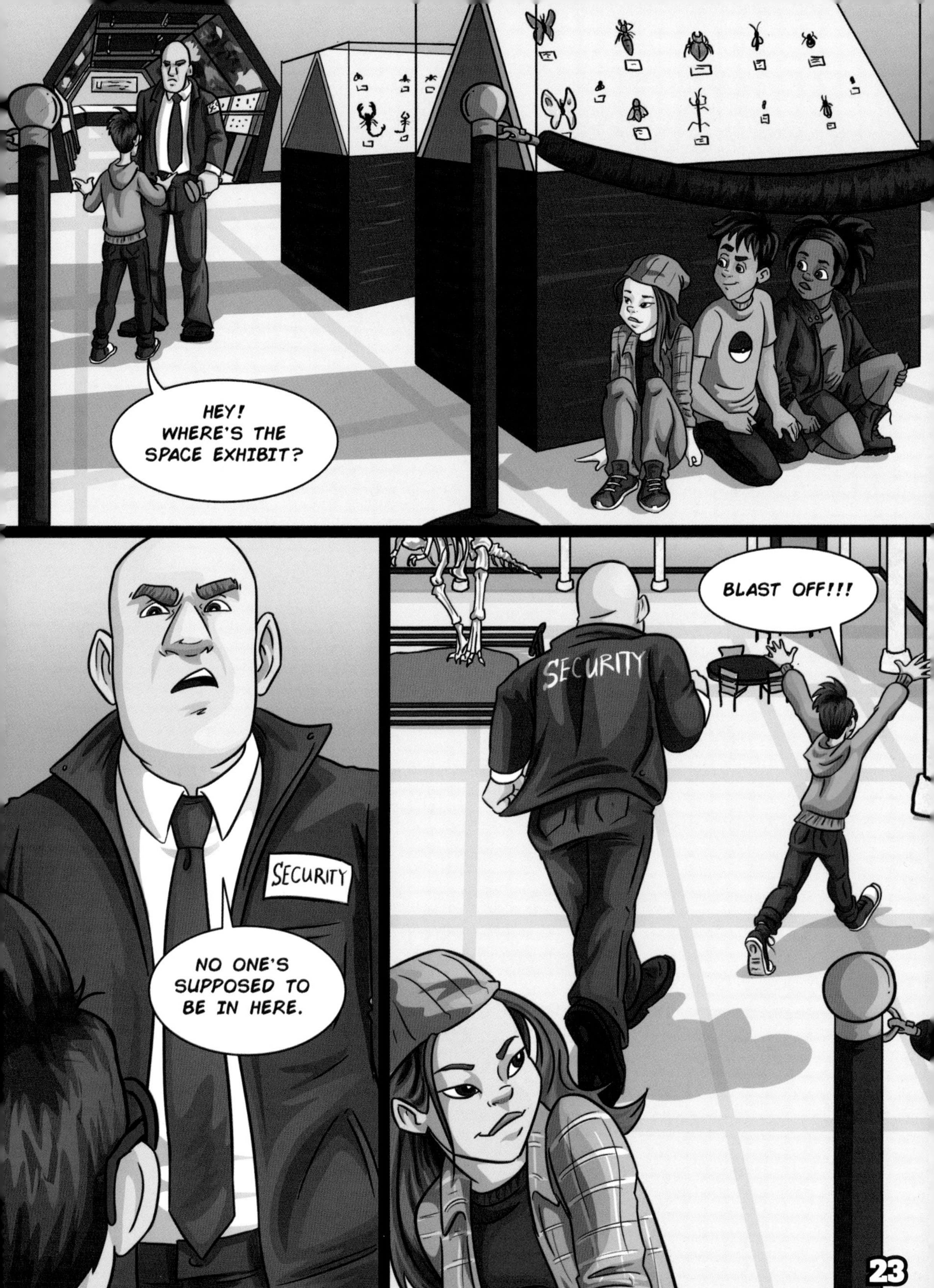
HEY! WHERE'S THE SPACE EXHIBIT?
SECURITY
NO ONE'S SUPPOSED TO BE IN HERE.
SECURITY
BLAST OFF!!!

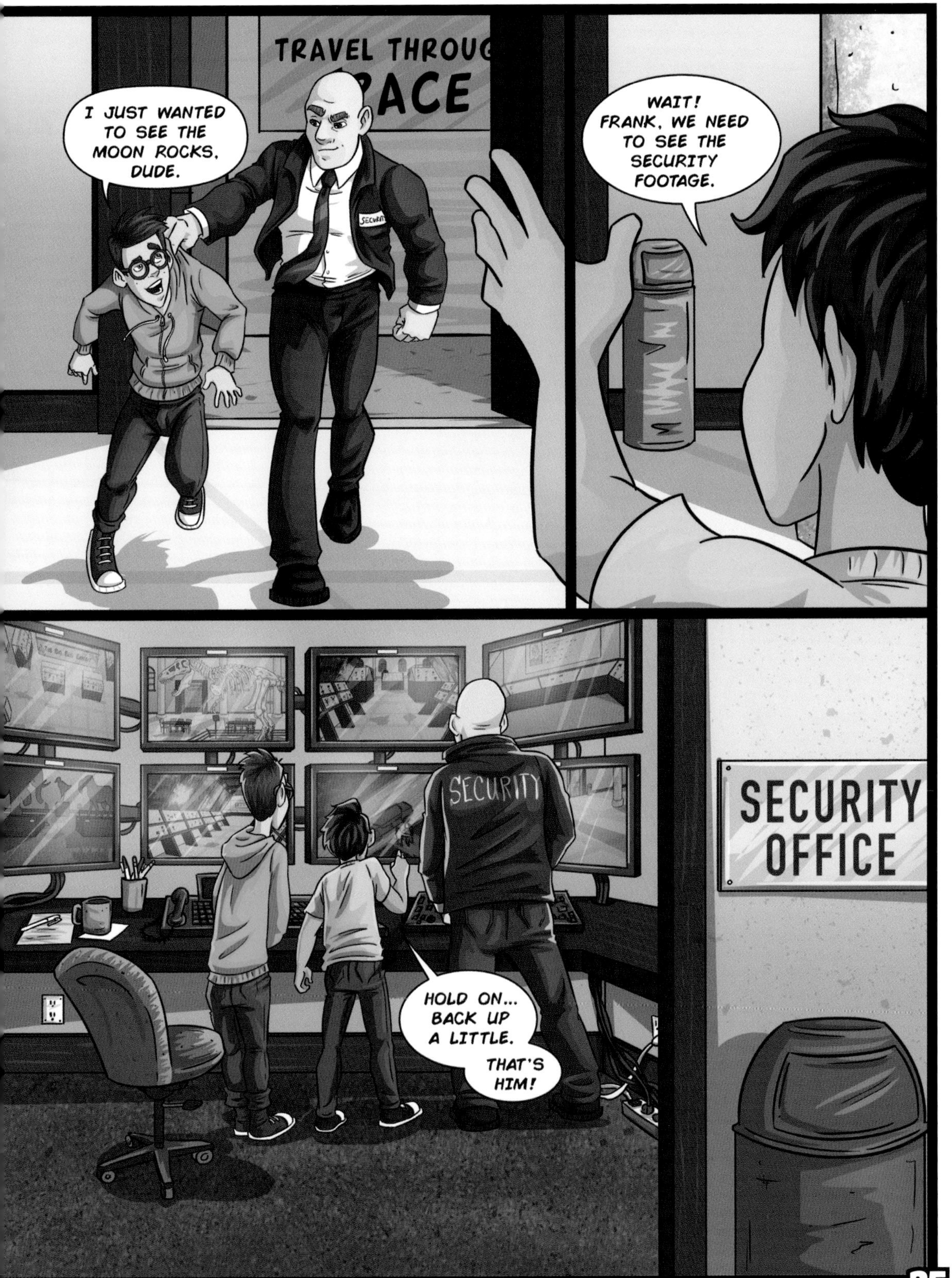
TRAVEL THROUG
PACE
I JUST WANTED TO SEE THE MOON ROCKS, DUDE.
SECURITY
WAIT! FRANK, WE NEED TO SEE THE SECURITY FOOTAGE.
SECURITY
SECURITY OFFICE
HOLD ON... BACK UP A LITTLE.
THAT'S HIM!

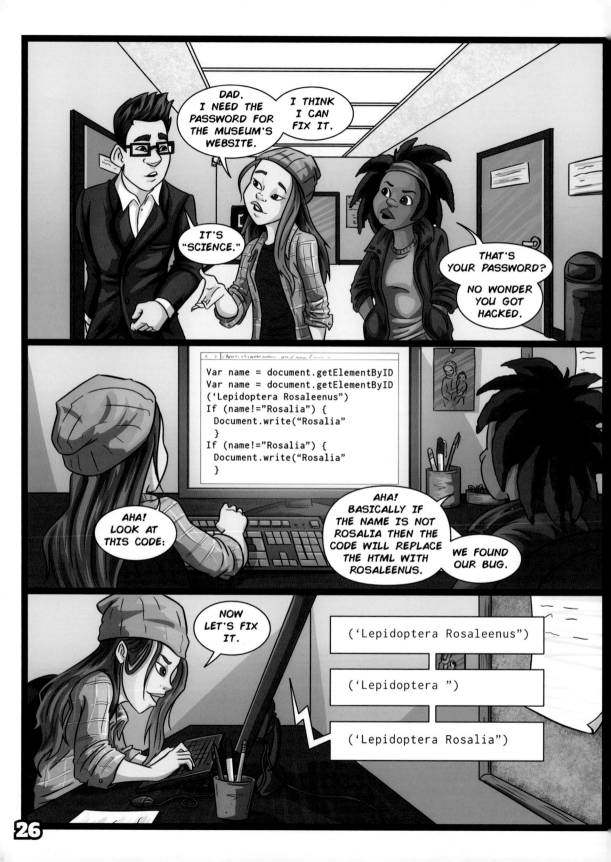

I'LL BRING THE MOTHS BACK ON ONE CONDITION.

ANYTHING!

YOU FIX THE LABEL ON THE EXHIBIT. SPELLING MATTERS.

I'D LIKE TO DO MORE THAN THAT...

CAN I WRITE AN ARTICLE ABOUT ROSALIA FOR THE SCIENCE MUSEUM WEBSITE? I THINK EVERYONE SHOULD KNOW HER STORY.

THAT WOULD BE...

OH NO! I FORGOT ABOUT THE WEBSITE. I'LL HAVE IT FIXED IMMEDIATELY.

MUSEUM
EMPLOYEE ENTRANCE

AUTHO
PERS

ALREADY FIXED! WE FIGURED OUT THE BUG.